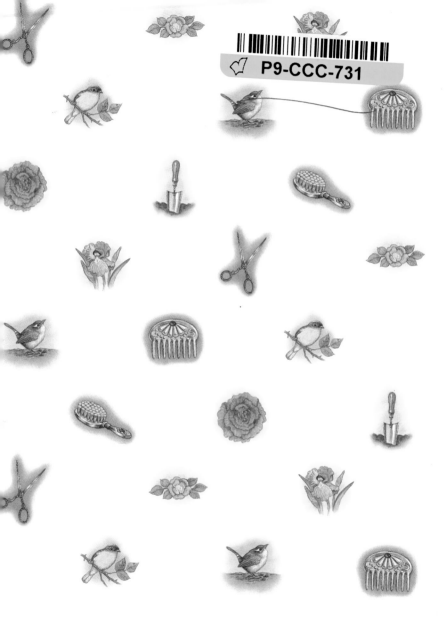

P9-CCC-731

Rapunzel

BY

The Brothers Grimm

Retold by Fiona Black

ILLUSTRATED BY

Victoria Lisi

ARIEL BOOKS

ANDREWS AND McMEEL
KANSAS CITY

Library of Congress Cataloging-in-Publication Data

Black, Fiona.
    Rapunzel / by the Brothers Grimm ; retold by Fiona Black ;
illustrated by Victoria Lisi.
      p.   cm.
    "Ariel Books."
    "Children's classics."
    Summary: A retelling of the Grimm fairy tale in which a beautiful
girl with long golden hair is imprisoned in a lonely tower by a witch.
    ISBN 0-8362-4924-0 : $6.95
    [1. Fairy tales. 2. Folklore—Germany.] I. Grimm, Jacob,
1785–1863. II. Grimm, Wilhelm, 1786–1859. III. Lisi, Victoria,
ill. IV. Rapunzel. English. V. Title.
PZ8.B557Rap   1992
[398.2]—dc20   92–14259
                                          CIP
                                          AC

Design: Susan Hood and Mike Hortens
Art Direction: Armand Eisen, Mike Hortens, and Julie Phillips
Art Production: Lynn Wine
Production: Julie Miller and Lisa Shadid

Rapunzel

There once lived a man and his wife who longed with all their hearts to have a child. At last, their wish was granted, and they were both glad.

Now, this couple's cottage had a window that overlooked a high stone wall. On the other side of the wall was a beautiful garden. This garden belonged to a wicked witch, and no one dared enter it.

One day, as the woman was gazing out the window and down into the garden, she happened to see some rapunzel.

The rapunzel leaves looked so fresh and green that the woman could not help wanting some. "How tasty it would be," she thought, and her mouth began to water. The woman knew she could not possibly have any of the witch's rapunzel, yet her longing for it grew stronger each day. At last, she became so pale and ill, her husband grew worried and asked her what was wrong.

"Ah," sighed the woman. "If I do not get some of the rapunzel from the witch's garden, I will surely die."

The man loved his wife and did not want her to become ill, so he decided he must get her the rapunzel. That night he climbed over the high stone wall and into the witch's garden. He plucked a handful of the rapunzel and quickly returned to his cottage.

The woman prepared a salad of the rapunzel and devoured it at once. But the rapunzel was so delicious that her desire only grew stronger. Her husband became afraid his wife would surely die if she could not have more rapunzel. So that night he once again climbed over the high stone wall and into the witch's garden.

Just as he was about to pick a handful of the rapunzel, he looked up to see the witch standing over him.

"How dare you, you thief!" the witch screamed at him. "Who do you think you are that you may steal rapunzel from my garden? I will make you pay dearly for this!"

The man fell to his knees and begged the witch for mercy. "I only stole the rapunzel for my dear wife," he cried. "I was afraid she would die if she could not have some, and she is about to bear our child."

When the witch heard about the child, she quickly grew calm.

"If what you say is true," she said, "you may take as much of my rapunzel as you like —on one condition! You must give me the child your wife is about to bear. Do not be afraid, I will take good care of your child and love it as a mother would."

Since there was nothing else he could do, the poor man agreed. When his wife gave birth to a girl, the witch took the child away.

The witch named the child Rapunzel and brought her up as her own. Rapunzel grew to be a most beautiful child. Even the blazing sun was in awe of her beauty, as was the shy silvery moon. When Rapunzel was twelve, the witch shut the girl in a high tower in the middle of the forest so no one would ever steal her away.

This tower had no door and no staircase. Instead, there was a single window at the very top. Whenever the witch wanted to visit Rapunzel, she would stand beneath this window and call up:

Rapunzel, Rapunzel,
Let down your hair!

Then Rapunzel, whose golden hair had never been cut, would wind her long, long braid around a

hook at the top of the
window. Next she would let
it tumble down to the
ground like a thick golden
rope. Then the witch
would climb up it as if
it were a ladder, and visit
with the girl.

One day a handsome young
prince was wandering in the
forest near Rapunzel's
tower. As the prince rode
past the tower, he heard
someone singing in a pure,
sweet voice. It was Rapunzel,
who often passed her lonely
days singing to herself.

The prince stopped to
listen. The singing was very
beautiful, but there was
something sad about it, too.

The prince found himself longing to meet the singer. He rode around the tower, looking for a door or a staircase, but he could find no way inside. At last, as it was growing dark, he rode home.

But the prince could not forget Rapunzel's singing. So he returned to the tower the very next day.

The prince was listening to Rapunzel's singing from behind a tree, when the old witch appeared. The prince watched, while she called up to the high window:

Rapunzel, Rapunzel,
Let down your hair!

The prince was amazed to see a braid of thick golden hair tumble out the window. Then he saw how the witch climbed up it into the tower.

"So that is how it is done," the prince said to himself.

As soon as the witch had climbed down and left, the prince ran to the tower. Then he called:

Rapunzel, Rapunzel,
Let down your hair!

Immediately Rapunzel let down her shining golden braid. The prince quickly

climbed up it and was soon standing in
Rapunzel's tower room.

At first, Rapunzel was very frightened of
the prince, for she had never seen a man
before. "Who are you?" she cried, backing
away.

The prince told Rapunzel his name. Then,
speaking to her gently, he said, "Your
singing so touched my heart that I could
not live in peace until I met you." As he
talked, Rapunzel began to lose her fear.
Indeed, he was a much more charming
companion than the witch.

After that, the prince visited Rapunzel
daily—but only in the evening since the
witch came during the day. Soon the two
young people grew to love each other. One

day the prince asked Rapunzel if she would marry him.

"Yes," Rapunzel replied. "I will gladly marry you. But first I must find a way to escape this tower."

Then Rapunzel told the prince that every time he visited, he must bring her some strong silk thread. "I will ply it into rope," she said. "And when it is finished, I will climb down from the tower and we can be together always."

Every day the prince brought a skein of silk thread. The witch suspected nothing. Finally, the rope was almost finished. Then, one day, when the witch came to see Rapunzel, the girl carelessly said, "Oh, Granny, why does it take you so much longer to climb up here than it does the prince?"

"What are you saying, you wicked child?" the witch snapped.

"Nothing," stammered the girl, realizing what she had done. But it was too late.

"I shut you away from the world, and still you have managed to betray me!" the witch shrieked.

The witch seized Rapunzel's one braid in her right hand and twisted it tight. Then with her left hand she took a pair of scissors and—*snip!*—she cut off Rapunzel's long golden braid.

Then the witch took the weeping Rapunzel far away to a barren desert. There she left the girl to live in poverty and misery.

That evening the prince came to the tower and called:

Rapunzel, Rapunzel,
Let down your hair!

The long shining hair came cascading down as usual, and the prince climbed up to the window.

Inside the tower he found waiting for him,
not his dear Rapunzel, but the wicked witch.

"Your beautiful songbird has flown away!"
the witch crooned mockingly. "The cat has
got her. And now the cat's going to scratch
out your eyes!"

Then she rushed at the prince. In his grief
and confusion, he leaped out the window.
Some bushes broke his fall and saved his life.
But their sharp thorns put out both his eyes.

For several years, the prince wandered
blind and almost out of his mind with

sorrow. By chance, he came to the desert place where Rapunzel was living.

He heard a pure, lovely, familiar voice singing a sad song. It was Rapunzel, and as the prince drew close, she recognized him. She threw her arms around his neck and began to weep.

When her tears fell into his eyes, his sight became clear again, and the prince saw his dear Rapunzel. He took her to his kingdom where they were married. And they both lived happily together.